Diary of NINJA BOY & Fartypants
Everybody hates Mondays

By Ninja Toe

Table of Contents

Chapter 1: Giants stink!

Of all the worst places in the world to be, there I was. This place took disgusting to a whole new level. My trusty sidekick, fartypants (my dog and best friend) and I, ninja boy, were deep inside Mount Hogsnort, sneaking past the smelly generators keeping the evil giant's lair cool.

We had to be as silent as possible, not only because that is the way of a true ninja, but also because the guards were sleeping, and it was much easier to pass by them than have to fight them all. Not that we would have lost to them or anything, but I'm just saying. It was much easier this way.

So there we were, focusing all our energy into being as quiet as possible. This was very difficult to do, because the guards were constantly farting in their sleep, so there were all these frt-vrt sounds blasting out of nowhere, making us both laugh and gag. Luckily, my specially designed ninja mask kept me safe from these toxic gases, but fartypants wasn't as lucky.

I could see his eyes starting to tear up, and he was crunching his nose, as if he wanted to sneeze but couldn't. I felt for the little guy, so I patted him gently on the nose and promised him a big treat once we get out of this whole stinky mess.

Suddenly, one of the guards released the smelliest, nastiest butt missile you could imagine! It smelled worse than cabbage with an angry skunk mixed together, and then thrown into the garbage for a few days. Yuck! It was like a million little green monsters digging for gold in your nose, and then pooping there!

Poor fartypants almost started coughing, but then held his breath a little and stayed quiet after shooting me a "what you gotten me into?" glare.

Whoa. That was a close one.

We managed to pass by the sleeping guards in the hallway, and reach a room that was locked with a smell detector. It looked like a big shiny panel, with lots of lights and buttons, and I think you were supposed to release a special gas into it for the door to open.

Probably one of the guards knew how to do it, but we couldn't risk waking just one up. Then, fartypants jumped onto the panel, wagged his tail, and burped (I always forget that he never brushes his teeth, so his breath doesn't smell as nice as mine.... that's at least what mom says).

Mom also says not to fart so much, that it's not considered very nice and polite, but then when I tell her it's her fault, she doesn't believe me. Next time she feeds me beans and cabbage, I'll show her.

But, back to fartypants opening the locked door. He just burped into the sensor and voila! The door opened. Every hero needed a sidekick as dependable as fartypants! I have to remember to get him double treats tonight.

What did we see when the door opened? My heart sank. There was Sarah in all her innocence and sweetness, shackled to the wall!

I instructed fartypants to keep a low profile. We had to plan this one out well. If all those things I saw aimed at Sarah were what I thought they were, then we were in deep trouble. I signaled at the stinkalators to fartypants, and he nodded his head. Yep, those were stinkalators alright.

Hidden behind a container, we could hear the giant yelling at Sarah, ordering her to tell him where I was. I could also see tears in sweet Sarah's eyes, because the smell was becoming unbearable. It was like a stinky hand poking your eyes. Saying it was unpleasant would be like saying that skunks have a special kind of smell.

The giant was getting impatient. And Sarah wouldn't be able to hold out much longer. We had to do something... anything!

I turned to fartypants, and started telling him about my plan. But, before I was able to say more than a couple of sentences, a siren started blasting. It was the alarm. "Danger! Danger! Smelly stranger!"

Then, I remembered: I hadn't given fartypants a bath in more than a week. No wonder the smell alarm went off! We knew it was now or never, so bravely, we jumped out into the open and showed the guards and the giant we were there to make trouble for them.

"After them!" The giant bellowed and a whole army of his guards fell upon us (who also by the way hadn't taken a shower probably longer than fartypants!). We were fighting every way we knew how: I tried to remember all my karate skills from school (the seven classes that I actually went to) and also, I remembered some movies where ninjas kicked butt.

Left leg up! Right leg kick! Left arm punch! Right arm squeeze! And of course, a lot of hyaaaaaaaa sounds. It really worked! Fartypants was right behind me: biting here and there, growling so scarily that some guards ran away in fear. Atta boy!

The guards kept shooting stinky air biscuits and throwing poisonous snot at us (Mom won't believe what happened to these clothes when I tell her), but a ninja is faster than the speed of light, so I managed to escape most.

I kept thinking about poor Sarah, my first ever possible girlfriend, and how she was chained to the wall, with the stinkalators aimed at her. This gave me additional power and I released such a thundering butt sneeze that all the leftover guards fell unconscious.

I dusted off my hands, turned toward the giant and said proudly: "That's how ninjas do it, you giant smelly turd. Now it's your turn!" At that, fartypants growled in agreement and we started approaching the evil giant, like a hawk preparing to grab a mouse in the field.

Chapter 2: Ready, Aim, Fire!

My right leg flew bravely through the air, aiming at the giant's head, but unfortunately it didn't get that far. The giant had a few ninja tricks up his sleeve, too and he twisted and turned a little, ending up with my poor head right underneath his sticky, smelly soggy, armpits!

"Blah! This smells so bad! Help, fartypants, help!" I was drowning in disgusting armpit smells, but good old trusty fartypants immediately came to the rescue. His sharp teeth flew like razors through the air, straight for the giant's butt, giving him such a painful bite that the giant let go of my head straightaway and I was able to think clearly again, free from those horrible smelly armpits of death.

What to do? I got it! Grab the stinkalator and blast the giant back to the dinosaur age and let him stink up all the world there! I managed to squeeze between fartypants who was keeping the giant away from us and the still knocked out guards, and get a hold of one of the biggest and smelliest stinkalators.

I pressed my index finger on the trigger and aimed it right at the giant. But not before I blew a small kiss to my lovely Sarah, letting her know that I'll get her down immediately, just needed to take out the trash first.

She smiled at me (oh, that Sarah...) and I know this meant that next day at school, I would get to sit next to her during lunch break. Heck, we might even walk home together and she might let me carry her books!

But, Manny, Manny... I mean, ninja boy, "Don't get ahead of yourself dude", I told myself. There's business to take care of now. Fun, games, and girls will have to wait. I turned back towards the giant and let out a manly laugh (like my Dad usually does).

"I have you now, you stinky hulk!" Yes, that sounded right. Dad could do better, but what's done is done.

The giant was just looking at me. I couldn't really say he was frightened of me (which is what I really wanted), but he was really frightened of fartypants. I guess dogs have to have their days, too.

So, I let fartypants have this one. But, only this one! Let Mom say now that I think only about myself, ha!

Back to my story. There we were, the three of us facing one another like cowboys in the Wild West, waiting for someone to draw. It's just that I was the only one with a weapon (apart from my super awesome ninja skills, of course). I held the stinkalator aimed at the giant.

There was no way I was letting him escape now. Now, that I had him. Finally, after all those years! But, every bad guy eventually loses to the good guy and here we were now. It looked like the end of a ninja episode. Who would be my next enemy? I wonder...

"It's over, giant. When I press this button, the stinkalator will make you so stinky you will never be able to go out in public and do any evil to anyone anymore!"

I had never been more proud of myself than at that moment. Fartypants gently brushed my knee with his ear, and I knew he felt the same. Ninja boy and fartypants! The best superhero duo this world has ever seen!

And, with these words in my mind, I pressed the trigger.

I don't know what was worse: the noise or the sound. It sounded like the wettest, stinkiest fart in the whole world. And the smell, ooooooh boy, the smell was something else!

My eyes started to tear up, fartypants started coughing, and the air became foggy and dense with stench. But I had to do it until the end.

I kept pressing and pressing, and suddenly, the farting noise turned into laughter. Silent at first, then louder and louder, until it reminded me of...

Chapter 3:
Did I just do that in class?

My classmates! I opened my eyes, and to my enormous embarrassment I realized I had been asleep all this time! And during science class with Mr. Shackleton!

What did I do? Did I talk in my sleep? Oh no! Did Sarah hear me? I turned to her then, but she wasn't laughing like the rest of them. She was looking at me, seriously. I don't know if this was worse or better.

Then I heard Mr. Shackleton's voice: "Mr. Monday, I would appreciate it if you didn't sleep in my classes. And also if you kept your giants and stinkalators to yourself, for the time being at least."

Well that last line really got my classmates going as if they didn't have enough to laugh at already. Shackleton would get his. One day.

"And Fanny farted, too! Farting Fanny! Hahahaha, Fanny has stinky panties..." I heard the combined cackles of Biff and Lonnie Fitz, the biggest jerks in the history of...jerks. They were the last thing I needed at a time like this.

Now, Sarah will never like me!

"EVERYONE hates Mondays...Monday! Mondays stink!" chanted Biff and Lonnie for the 100 thousandth time since they thought of it. They thought they were so funny making fun of my last name like that.

I'd always hated my name. Manny Monday? What were my parents thinking? I'd have much rather it had occurred to them to name me something cool like Mad Dog Monday, anything but Manny!

I turned as red as a tomato, you know those very red ones, very sweet, juicy and delicious, that Mom gets from the market in the summertime? Yeah, that's how I felt. Red, but not very sweet or delicious.

Everyone was laughing and I felt just about the worst I had ever felt. I almost wished that I never turn into ninja boy again. But I know that wouldn't be fair to the rest of the world, because who will fight the bad guys then?

I wished I was home with Dad. He always knew what to say to make everything better.

"Alright, alright," the voice of Mr. Shackleton tried to calm everyone down. About time, I thought. "Let's continue where we left off before... the alarm went off." Even he giggled to himself when he said that. But, we managed to continue the class.

Of course, I was in no mood for science and could hardly wait for my last class of the day.

Chapter 4:
From Bad to Worse, to Worstest

The day was about to get even worse. I had forgotten all about the afternoon's baseball try outs. Ugggh! I got embarrassed once already, now I had to do it again? Seriously, could this day get any more horrible?

I tried to remember what my Dad had told me before about baseball. Keep your eyes on the ball, son. Be one with the ball, son. And your bat is an extension of your arm and hand, son. It all makes so much sense when he talks, but that's because he loves baseball! Me? Not so much. But I had to give it a go. For Dad.

So I got ready and went out onto the field. The sun was shining. The birds were singing. I almost forgot about my big embarrassment earlier that day. But as always, more was yet to come.

Standing in the middle of the field, ready to swing, I noticed the giant's henchmen rushing down at me from the bleachers. Really? Now? I squinted, trying to see more clearly. Yep. It was them alright. They looked angry and out for revenge. I didn't have my trusty fartypants by my side, but ninja boy is no coward! I'll show them what I'm made of! I dropped my bat right then and there, and rushed towards them.

Then all of a sudden, they started throwing smelly shuriken stars at me! As they flew through the air, they left a foggy green trail. Poisonous shuriken stars! I knew I couldn't let them touch my skin, otherwise I'd become smelly forever! So, I started running across the field, avoiding the flying stars, out to get me.

Left and right, I ran until finally, one of them hit me right on the forehead and that was the last thing I remembered, before I fell to the ground, with a loud thump.

"Earth to Monday! Earth to Monday!" I kept hearing, as if from a cave or something. "Throw some water on him!" "No, shake him up a little!" "Leave him alone, he's coming around!" "Is he alright?" "Should we call the nurse?"

I heard several voices, until finally, I heard the coach. "Monday, Monday! Are you alright?" I had a booming headache from the ball that hit me, but otherwise I was okay. "You gave us quite a scare, son. Are you sure you're alright?" The coach sounded really worried, but I nodded and smiled back in agreement. Then the coach started scratching his head, as if he was feeling uncomfortable.

"You know, Monday...usually the players aren't supposed to run away from the ball. That's not really how the game is played." There was giggling in the background. Lonnie and Biff, I bet. "And you're not supposed to throw the bat away, you use it to actually hit the balls. Do you understand what I'm saying?"

I felt like a baby being told how to eat soup with a spoon. Of course I knew what I had to do. I just got lost in my thoughts, that's all!

"I'm sorry, coach." I had to apologize and convince him to give me another chance. "I have no idea what happened. It won't happen again, though. Would it be alright if I tried out again tomorrow?" I saw the expression on the coach's face, but he was always a nice guy. That's why everyone liked him.

"Well, alright, Manny. If you feel you're up for it." I almost yelled "of course I was" to the coach, but I saw it was unnecessary. I thanked him for being so nice and understanding, and hoped that the day would finally be over. I just couldn't take anymore.

Chapter 5: Okay, Dad

When I returned home that day, the first person I saw was Dad. I was hoping it'd be my Mom, not because I love her more, but because I was really disappointed with what happened during the baseball try out and I didn't know how to explain it to my Dad that I don't really want to play baseball. I can't play and I don't want to. Easy as that. I just wish I could say this to his face.

"Hey there, little man!" The smile on my Dad's face was huge. There was probably a baseball game on and his team is either winning or has won. It didn't matter which one.

"How did the baseball try out go today, champ?" I looked down at my sneakers, dirty from running across the baseball field. "Weeeeeeell, you see, Dad…" I started to say, but then he interrupted me.

"It'd mean the world to me if you got on the team, Manny." Then, he looked somewhere far away, as if he was remembering something very nice, something I wasn't a part of, but he was still trying to share it with me. "Have I ever told you that I was on my school baseball team? And we were winners, all the way!" My Dad put his heavy hand on my shoulder. He always did this when he wanted to let me know how much he loves me. Today, his hand felt heavier than it actually is. As if somehow, I didn't deserve to have it there.

"Don't worry, son. If you give it your best shot, I'm sure you'll succeed in getting on the team. And I'll be there in the front lines with Mom, to cheer you on, champ." I felt uneasy, but I managed to smile at him. I mean, what else was there to say?

Chapter 6: Here we go again

So, there I was the following day, on the baseball field. Was I ready, you ask? Well. As ready as I'd ever be, I guess. The coach was there of course, first worried if I was alright to try out, but then he was his old cheerful self again, cracking jokes with everyone. The whole team was also there, including those big, mean oafs Biff and Lonnie.

I wished they would disappear in the fog of a stinkalator, but unfortunately this wasn't one of those ninja days. Wouldn't it be awesome if all days were ninja days? But, of course they aren't. This can't be, so we have to survive, maybe even enjoy the regular days and look forward to and enjoy even more those special ninja days.

But, back to the baseball field and my non-ninja day. I couldn't wish Biff and Lonnie away, no matter how much I wanted it. I guess wishful thinking doesn't really work that way. Even though, Mom did tell me that all have to do is wish really hard for something I want and it is bound to come true (thanks, Mom!).

So, I really tried hard this time. Like I do when I'm a ninja, I tried to remember everything I knew about baseball and use it right then and there. I focused on the ball, I held my bat as tightly as that stink gun from the day before, but nothing.

I sucked! I sucked so bad that Biff and Lonnie were laughing the whole time, calling me horrible names and booing me. They were even on the ground one time, wallowing in dirt and laughing their butts off at the fifty fifth ball I swung at and missed. How did it feel? Well, how do you think it felt?

"Nice whiff, Monday! Don't fart, Fanny!" I heard them gleefully cheer.

That night when I went to bed, I started thinking. Maybe I would have done better at the try out, if only those two pug-nosed stinker brutes Biff and Lonnie, weren't making so much fun of me. I was already nervous enough, but they kept calling me names and being even meaner to me than usual. That was too much. And I thought to myself: sweet, I mean stinky, revenge. I closed my eyes, patted fartypants on the head, hearing him softly fart in reply, and fell asleep.

So I devised a wicked plan for the following school day: I would use that old fart pillow we've got, the one we don't play with anymore, so no one would notice it's missing, disguise it somehow and put it on Biff's chair at school. See, I knew that Biff was always the last one to arrive to school (even though he lives a ten minutes' walk from the actual school). Sometimes he even arrives after the teachers! Which in this case, would be the cherry on top.

I arrived at school feeling very happy that day. It seemed that it was all going my way and finally, some luck for good ole Manny Monday. Everything was happening according to my awesome plan. I positioned the fart pillow just right, and Biff arrived just after the teachers, rushing inside with his big red bloated cheeks.

Everything seemed to happen in slow motion after that. I was so nervous! He approached his desk...but turned back around to punch a kid in the back. Biff came back to the desk looking pretty proud of himself, scooted in and finally, plopped right down on my booby trap and just then an enormous fart noise ripped through every corner of the classroom. The ground even seemed to shake!

After the initial shock and the wide open eyes of all our classmates, we all burst into laughter! Voices spread out through the classroom: "Biff farted! Oh my gosh! No way! Really?" For the first time ever, I actually participated in the laughing part.

Chapter 7: Ninja Revenge!

But, I wasn't finished for the day. I waited patiently for school to be over, and decided to go home the roundabout way, past Biff and Lonnie's house. I still had a score to settle.

Once I locked on to my target (Lonnie with his girlfriend, Maya) I followed them from a safe distance. Slowly, but surely I got closer and closer, until I was so close I could hear what they were talking about. "... and so I told him to give me all his lunch money, before I beat the crap out of him."

Lonnie was bragging to Maya about his bully business. I had no idea what she saw in him, but then again, I didn't really care. I had my heavenly Sarah, after all. I started walking faster, passing by them, and then whistled silently, without anyone hearing.

All of a sudden, a loud and very horrible farting noise was heard. All three of us stopped. I turned around, pretending to be shocked. Maya let go of Lonnie's hand. I started. "Lonnie! You didn't! Seriously! It smells like dead skunks out here!" I waved my hand in front of my nose, trying to make the stench in the air go away.

"Seriously, Lonnie! And in front of Maya? What were you thinking?" Maya was furious, while Lonnie was still in shock, having no idea what had happened. Then, Maya stormed away from Lonnie, and I rushed past him, making sure I was out of his reach. "Yeah Lonnie, didn't your mom ever teach you it's not nice to fart in front of girls?" I started laughing, just like he was during my pitiful baseball tryout, and whistled again. There he was. My dog fartypants, lollygagging behind a tree, until I called out to him and we both rushed home. It's a good thing I fed him beans this morning!

Chapter 8: Lazy afternoons and sneak attacks

That afternoon, I decided to give baseball one last go. I even called Arbuckle, being my best friend and all, hoping he could help me. Now, Arbuckle is not a jock, and neither am I, but I was thinking I could at least practice a little with him. Just so that I don't suck so much next time. That was the least I could do.

So, Arbuckle and I threw the ball around a little, but no matter how much we tried, we just couldn't pull it off. I mean, if you can't do it, you can't do it. I've tried (oh, how I tried!), and I don't like it. Not one bit. It's just how things are. Baseball isn't for me. Something else is. Something different must be, because we're all different. Yeah, that sounded like a good thing to tell my Dad. Hopefully, he'd understand.

So, after almost an entire hour trying to hit and throw and looking more like dying leeches than baseball players, Arbuckle and I got super bored. It was already dinner time, and Arbuckle never missed dinner so he went home while I decided to stay outside a little longer and meditate about some ninja stuff.

Mom said meditation calms the mind and a ninja should have a calm mind to be able to fight all those bad guys. She has very good ideas sometimes, my Mom. I had no idea how exactly to do this meditation thing the right way, so I just sat on the grass a little and thought about Sarah. Thinking about her makes me smile and she calms my mind, so I guess for me, Sarah is meditation. I thought about her pigtails, how her hair smells like apples and how she has those glittery stickers on her notebooks. They are girly and I don't like them, but everything Sarah has and does is okay in my book.

Suddenly, fartypants came running towards me, barking madly. "What is it, boy?" I asked, jumping to my feet immediately, ready for action. My ninja skills have always allowed me to understand everything fartypants tells me. In other words, I speak dog language. Well, just fartypants language because he was no ordinary dog.

"Sarah has been captured again by the evil giant? Not on our watch!" I managed to change into my ninja suit in the blink of an eye, and I was ready to fight for Sarah. I grabbed the sword that was lying on the ground (it didn't matter that it was wooden and kinda dull), but in my ninja hands, it became the deadliest weapon in the world. After all, a well-armed ninja is a deadly ninja.

And, then, there they were. Hoards of the giant's henchmen (with ninjas this time!) swarmed our garden, like angry bees, and I knew that I couldn't let them enter the house and hurt Mom and Dad. "Keep the entrance safe, fartypants!" I yelled and drove straight into the pile of evil henchmen like an arrow hitting bull's eye. I was cutting down ninjas and henchmen like trees, and fartypants was using his wicked biting skills. One by one, they kept falling down. Neither of us rested for a second, defending our home and hoping we'd reach delicate Sarah in time.

I was jumping around everywhere, cutting the air as well as our enemies with my razor sharp sword, kicking them down with my super powerful ninja kicks and karate chops. Hyaaah! Soon after, our back yard was covered with evil villains knocked unconscious. I wondered what Mom would say if she saw them? But, I'd make sure that never happens, because I would always keep my Mom and Dad safe. And now, it was time to go save Sarah!

It is strange that we hadn't noticed it sooner, but the giant was actually keeping Sarah prisoner behind our big oak tree. When I saw her, I immediately ran to save her. As always, she barely looked me in the face, because she is a very shy girl, but she smiled, and I saw that her cheeks became rosy.

I made sure that her hands and feet were free, that she wasn't hurt and was safe, and then I turned my attention back to the evil giant who looked an awful lot like Mr. Shackleton.

"You monster!" I yelled at him, angry that he dared kidnap my Sarah...again. But before fartypants and I managed to do anything to him, he laughed in a very wicked way, (like bad guys do in movies) and said "This isn't the last you'll see of me, ninja boy..." T

Then he disappeared in a stinky cloud of green smoke, and all I was left with was fartypants and a whole bunch of cut down sunflowers, all over mom's garden.

I turned around to where Sarah was standing, but she wasn't there anymore. My super awesome ninja skills then made me remember: she was transported back home through the use of an invisible power, which only we ninjas have. I also remembered that she actually did look me in the eyes once, and promised that soon, she would give me a reward for being so brave and saving her. Even fartypants got a little something: she petted him on the head, which made him wag his tail and fart even more cheerfully than usual.

Was I happy? Absolutely. Was I scared what Mom was going to say about me chopping down her sunflowers in a valiant defense of our home? You bet. But knowing that I managed to save fair Sarah again made me not fear anything.

Chapter 9: Understandings and border wars

Then, it hit me. I was supposed to be practicing baseball and not have one of my ninja adventures! This thought made me sad, because I let my Dad down. I'd never get on the team, and nothing would have made him happier.

Just then, his voice called out to me from the window. "Manny! Could you come inside for a second?" Uh-oh. What did that mean? I didn't really want to have any conversations with my Dad right now, but I couldn't say no. So, I went inside.

Dad was sitting on the sofa, asking me to join him. "I see you've been playing ninjas again, son." He said. It didn't look like he was in a bad mood. But then again, that's not what I was afraid of more than anything. "Yeah." I couldn't look him in the eyes.

"Arbuckle came and we practiced some baseball, but then he had to go home." Dad smiled. "I see. And do you enjoy playing baseball?" A trick question? What did that mean? I didn't know how to reply in the beginning. "Well Dad... to tell you the truth, not really." I was looking at the ground and not at my Dad. "Why not?" How do I explain this to him?

"Well, you see Dad, I'm not very good at baseball, because I don't really like it. I like other things." Dad nodded. "You can look at me, son. The fact that we are having a serious conversation doesn't mean I'm upset with you." His voice was soft and it gave me the strength to look him straight in the eyes. Like he had taught me.

"Atta boy. Now, Manny, why didn't you tell me about this before?" Somehow, it got easier to talk to him from then on. "I didn't want to disappoint you." Dad shifted his place, and sat next to me. "You could never disappoint me, Manny. And just because you don't like something I do, doesn't change the way we feel about each other. I want you to do what you enjoy and go after your dreams, not mine or your Mom's. Do you understand?" He put a hand on my shoulder. His hand never felt lighter, and more loving. "I do!" I smiled back and gave him a big hug.

Then, he ruffled my hair and finished, "Now, get out, you little scamp!" After this very serious conversation with my Dad, I felt like I was flying. I even felt proud to be a Monday. But the best part was that I was off the hook for baseball...thank goodness! Mom then yelled that dinner would be ready soon, but I was already out, trying to find my trusty sidekick.

"Fartypants! Oh, fartypants! Where are you, boy?" I yelled and whistled. The sunflowers were still resting on the ground, like fallen soldiers. They reminded me of my battle, of how brave fartypants and I were, and of course, how Sarah promised to reward me soon for my bravery. Yes, being a ninja is pretty awesome.

All of a sudden, I heard growling from behind the house. I rushed there, and to my surprise there was fartypants, running after the neighbor's dog. Why, you might ask? Well, let me point you to the right direction. Yep, right over there, to the left of the house. Do you see that? Yes, it's what you think it is. The neighbor's dog left a stinky little "present" for us, and fartypants was just trying to show him who's the boss around here and who makes the rules. This is not a very nice thing to do, not even for a dog. No, no, no.

I took a deep sigh, and pulled down my ninja disguise. Danger was definitely in the air. I guess a ninja's job is never done.

The End

.....or is it?

Be sure to check out the next adventure of NINJA BOY and fartypants in...

Book 2: Attack of the Bathroom Pirates

About the Author

Ninja Toe

Nobody knows whose toe, ninja toe is. Or if he even is someone's toe. Nobody knows much about ninja toe at all really. He's never been seen. This photo is the only visual proof we have. He sure can write though. If you've read this book, it would pay to be on the lookout for ninja toe. It's been said that he enjoys checking in on his readers personally, to make sure that they're worthy of reading his books. And don't even think about leaving ninja toe a bad review. The aftermath of such a foolish mistake would be ugly and painful. Enemies of ninja toe don't seem to stick around long. Nor do enemies of ninja toe's many fans. Who IS ninja toe? Secret avenger? Ninja? Toe? Author? You might think it silly that a toe could write a book or be a ninja. But it would be smart to not question ninja toe. Seriously. Don't do it. He's a ninja. And a toe.

About the Illustrator

Dushko Zafirovski

Dushko is from Macedonia. Do you know where that is? I'll bet you don't! Have you ever seen a mightier mustache? It's magnificent even by Macedonian mustache standards. So is his illustrating. Dushko doesn't mind if you simply call him The Dush, but be warned. He's good friends with Ninja Toe. So tread lightly my friend!

Made in the USA
San Bernardino, CA
09 September 2016